THE STUDENTS OF SNOW

THE STUDENTS OF SNOW

Jane Flanders

THE UNIVERSITY OF MASSACHUSETTS PRESS AMHERST 1982

ALSO BY JANE FLANDERS

Leaving and Coming Back

 Printed in the United States of America
Library of Congress Cataloging in Publication Data
Flanders, Jane, 1940–
The students of snow.
I. Title.
DS3556.L347S8 1982 811'.54 82-8461
ISBN 0-87023-378-5 AACR2
ISBN -379-3 (pbk.)

The Students of Snow has been published with the support of the Literature Program of the National Endowment for the Arts, a federal agency, to whom acknowledgment is gratefully made.

Grateful acknowledgment is made to the following journals for permission to reprint poems that originally appeared in their pages:
The Atlantic Monthly, August Philosophers; *The Chowder Review*, After Manet, His Niche, In the Pergola, The Students of Snow, Tante Fräni's Handkerchief, Ukiyo-e; *Commonweal*, The Butter Road; *Confrontations*, Twigs; *John O'Hara Journal*, Morning and We Are Householders, Model Victory; *The Nation*, Moss, Picasso's Blue Period, Spring Fire, Stasis; *The New Jersey Poetry Journal*, La Belle Chatte, Vanishing Point; *The New Republic*, The Tipsy Woman; *Poetry Now*, Special Friends; *Shenandoah*, That Recent Invention, the Wheel; *Sun Dog*, Sunflowers; *West Branch*, Heavenly Bodies, The Scholar's Stone Garden, I Have Beheld Such Splendors; *Wind*, Peacetime; Grandfather Mountain, Ice Age, The Water-Garden, Giverny, Your Name in Greek, are reprinted from *The Literary Review* 23, no. 3 (1980) and 25, no. 3 (1982), published by Fairleigh Dickinson University; The Portrait is reprinted from *The Massachusetts Review* 22, no. 2 (1981), © 1981 The Massachusetts Review, Inc; Snowbirds is reprinted from *New England Review* 4, no. 1 (Season 1981), © 1981 by Jane Flanders; Wild Asters and Late Report from Miss Harriet Robinson's Third Grade appeared in *Poetry* © 1979 and 1982, The Modern Poetry Association; The Students of Snow appeared in *The Pushcart Prize, 5: The Best of the Small Presses.*

FOR STEVE

I MIGRATIONS TO SOLITUDE

II THE SMOKE OF THE VILLAGES

Yet, under the migrations to solitude,
There remained the smoke of the villages.

—WALLACE STEVENS

I MIGRATIONS TO SOLITUDE

THE STUDENTS OF SNOW

The students of snow will tell you few flakes
attain perfect symmetry.
There are many irregular forms, icy
spicules, frostlike sprigs,
forms due to twinning.

They may be needle-shaped, columnar,
three-sided or quadrilateral. Even the whiteness
is illusory. They can tell you
of red and green
snow, of the fabulous blue snow
that saved Nebraska.

The students of snow would never say
snowflakes are unique.
They would only admit they have never
seen two alike.
And no two students of snow are alike: Professor
Squinabol, Mrs. Chickering,
Herr Sigsun, and "Snowflake"
Bentley, the first microphotographer of snow,
bending almost invisibly
over his slide in a white smock.

Even in old age the students of snow
adore bad weather,
but they will tell you, the light
glinting off their spectacles, snow can fall
even from clear skies.
They say that true
crystals are not formed from clouds,
but from the unseen molecules within them.
And then they cease to speak, caught up
in the study of silence, transparency,
the radiant wedding of nebulae.

MOSS

Moss is one of the old ones.
Before fish crawled out of sea,
moss did it, from eon to eon,
the first green thing that learned to walk.

Before flower, came moss.
Before grass.
Before tree—moss *was* tree.
Before moss was only sun, wind, rain.

Moss is direction-giver,
the quiet one
on the other side of the trunk.

Every day moss is a different green.

If you stuff your pillow with moss
you will dream of first love.
If you eat moss, you will sprout horns.
If you conceive while lying on moss
your child will live hundreds of years.

Moss is the fur of stones.

Moss married itself and has never
regretted it, spitting its children out
like teeth.

Gradually moss has learned humility.

Mothers line cradles with moss.
Birds build their nests with it.
Men cram it in chinks to keep out the cold.
The world is sustained by moss.

Even moss, with its tiny spears,
is always afraid.

Moss means to go on just the same.

THE TIPSY WOMAN
(After Manet)

She was not always so.

In fact, just this morning,
waking up between grey sheets,
she saw the world as it is—
makeshift, full of endless detail.

After the first drink
her blood began to hazard the rapids:
she combed her hair.

After the second drink she could say,
to nobody in particular:
"Shall I wear the bombazine or
peau de soie? And which
of my hundreds of bonnets?"

After the third drink
she chose the black straw
and made her way carefully down the stairs
with their carpet of monstrous roses,
through beveled-glass doors and out
into the street.

It was Paris in the seventies.
There was still too much of everything.
She winced at the light
and turned towards a café.

After the anisette
she will permit us to find her,
dreaming over a plum in a glass dish.

GETTYSBURG, 1981

After the war, we walked the battlefield.
It was November. Monuments were cold
to the touch, guns and fences frozen in place.

All was as it should be in that season—
wind, cows, leaves on the ground, empty
woods crisscrossed by hawks, night coming early.

During the war the days were long. Corn
reached to a man's breast. In a farmhouse officers
sat up late. Women prepared for the harvest.

We weren't there long. Our children climbed on rocks,
crept under them, called them caves and hideouts,
never having heard of cenotaphs.

We saw meadows, hills, railroad cuts
someone defended and someone attacked, barns
with bullet holes. Alone on a ridge at dusk

we watched the sky turn red and seep away.
The children were suddenly quarrelsome and hungry.
This was after the war, long after the war.

WILD ASTERS

The asters quiver like palsied heads
tinged with lavender.
Every year at this time they come down with the shakes.
August fever. It has something to do with
the way insects approach them, hurriedly,
on frayed wings. And the wind
forces them into postures of forgetfulness.
There is warmth but no future here.
No time to grow young again and tour the Grecian isles.
They nod in sunny spots, where the
pebbles remind them of bone china,
discussing their daughters, the clouds,
and their sons, the tall trees.

PICASSO'S BLUE PERIOD

blue-grey eyes
your Yugoslavian shirt
sea-water the color of moss agates
cerulean sky

white paper with thin blue lines
the plum-colored bruise on your neck
your name in blue script

borage, flax, forget-me-nots
pale horizon
the blue-green veins in your hand

today the sea is indigo
the hills drift away like smoke
your milky breasts
larkspur, hyacinth
your lips
delphinium

and the sky is full of sapphires

cobalt streets
lilacs, lavender
a blue wash over everything

the ship sails off on an azure field
steel-blue shadows
turquoise fish
under the ashen trees

is that all?

no, the faint blue aura of your smile
tidal pools
aquamarines, lapis lazuli

there are bachelor's buttons in the garden

is that all?

no, I remember your blue thighs
blue china
treacherous blue-black water

HEAVENLY BODIES

It is always night in the outhouse
and smells like a pig sty.
I unbutton my sunsuit, pull it down
and perch, feet dangling, on the rim of
the abyss beside a prewar Sears catalogue.
The seat is silky from the buttocks of my
aunt and uncle and grown-up cousin.
I imagine them grunting away
year after year, in all weathers,
emptying themselves into this bowl
of sticky soup the flies
love so well. Sighing,
I let my urine float downward, outward
through space, marking this spot as mine
too, knowing myself related to the universe
in yet another unspeakable way.

STASIS

Something out there
refuses to give up.

Always air rises
into the blue or gray
or heliotrope.

A leaf shuffles
across the street.

Under the ice
the pond steams and stirs.

This nameless season
that grips us from within

is far colder, darker,
very still.

GRANDFATHER MOUNTAIN

We're trying to keep in touch, old man,
but it's hard now
that you've gone to live with
the elements. How adamant
you have become, since you gave up tears
and let the rain take care of it,
how set in your ways,
since the wind learned to breathe for you.

We don't know what to make of you,
standing beside the lake, year after year,
displaying your nakedness,
no periwig, no place for your medals,
only the deer coming to drink
and foxes towards evening.

The news we bring from the world is this:
our lives are going
as well as can be expected. The imprint
of your hand has gradually
softened and bled away.
It is pleasant to be on our own, but lonely.
We still tell your stories:
"How Grandfather Harnessed the Lightning,"
"How Grandfather Horsewhipped the Sun."

They say you are living more and more
in the past, as is natural,
now that your eyes are boulders,
your ears precipices of silence,
your tongue a slippery slide.
Just as well.
Better ignore the traffic of clouds.
Better go back to your sweet-faced youth
when Orion was just a kid
and the Pleiades were pretty girls
living by the sea,
letting the sea wash over them.

Mt. Colden
August 1979

LA BELLE CHATTE
(After a Child's Drawing)

The beautiful cat, in her nightgown of stars,
is ready for bed. In her red bow,
in her polka-dot cap she pauses
before her vanity—earrings and necklaces
shimmer beneath her sighs.

The moon swings on a fragile nail.
The beautiful cat's bed drifts towards the door.
Where is she going? What dream awaits her?
(In the kitchen nothing is happening.
The oven is empty. Fish float in the sink.)

SNOWBIRDS

A child fell asleep in the snow.
That's how we think of it—
as if it happened ages ago
anywhere but here.

(The boy keeps trying to tell us
but we don't want to know.)

She just lay down in the light,
in the bright
snow that loved her.

She wanted a dress so pure
no one else could marry her,
wanted to strike a perfect pose
forever.

(The boy says no,
it was not like that at all.)

Other children are building forts
and snowmen. They keep falling
down and getting back up.
Blood suffuses their cheeks.

(Only the boy understands
what falls from the sky must be
embraced.)

Think of the snow as a bed.

(Someone has already said that.)

Think of the snow as a white room,
silent except for the magnified
beating of a heart.
Think of white as the presence of
everything.

What is that strange
twittering in the trees?

(The boy is calling her name
but we say, "Please,
she needs her sleep in the snow.")

And all over town
snow has drifted into the shape
of a familiar face.

(We have not taken into account
the boy's version. That it snowed
afterwards. How she whirled out
into the path of a bus, though he
called her back. The snow came
afterwards, he says,
filling streets to the brim,
till children were safe.

If you lie very still,
you can hear them everywhere,
singing in the snow.)

for Piers and Claudia Bocock

HOW SHE WAKES

Like a small boat
far from shore
with only the breath
of our voices
making the sails flutter
and slap. She floats,
closing her eyes
to the sun,
on aimless waves.

Imagine birds
coming back after
hundreds of years.
They do not remember
much, except that the shadows
point a certain
way, or so they were told
by their spirit
ancestors. Hardly enough,
one would think,
and yet,
one day we hear a new
song, find a white
feather in the grass.

Or think of a seed
thrusting up from under the ice,
its roots feeling for
stones, mud, anything.
Roots, that have never
heard of a flower.
(Flowers?
Yes, tell us—there were such
bright, mischievous
creatures, once,
were there not?)

And you, who have feared
so many springs
would never come,

surely you
have learned something
which could be of use to you now,
you who also slept
in the womb,
clutching some tiny
talisman in your fist,
and rose so easily,
like a dancer, on your toes.

She drifts. She dreams
she is that grain of wheat
which must die before
harvest. She waits,
like stone, for the sculptor
to claim her heart.

Now the flute beckons
with hollow tongue.
A vine on the jungle floor
inches towards dark
trunks to be raised
to light.
Trust her.
Believe in her,
how she is waking—here,
there, with such
delicacy,
such infinite restraint.

again, for Claudia

THE PORTRAIT

"I find that I have painted my life . . . without knowing."
—Georgia O'Keeffe

What I saw had so little to do with me,
or so I thought. I was the lens,
the clear glass through which all passed,
or was I a mirror, a still, sullen pool?
A delicate instrument? A recording device?
I could have accepted that.

Sometimes, to escape from the brightness
I closed my eyes and felt my way through rocks,
shells, driftwood, seeking that sixth sense
of the blind. Or tasted fruit as if I were nothing
but lips, tongue, gullet. But the gold juice,
the air I sucked up pure, appeared on canvas
tinged with blood. No one had ever seen such
fleshy flowers, such landscapes of bones.

KINDERHOOK: THE STREAM TALKS BACK

What, would you have me
grow older, like you? Nonsense.
I'm still playing Poohsticks,
picking away at the banks, hiding
in secret shifting pools.

Would you praise my clarity?
Go ahead, it's nothing to me.
I would as soon be called
muddy, careless, ignorant,
not to be trifled with.

Next you will be "entranced
by my bubbling laughter"
as I "skip over stones."
What a hold They have on you.
"Cool and refreshing," indeed.

I'm cold as death. Fah!
I'm not like music either.
Tell a fish it's swimming
through a symphony—tell a fish
anything, it won't believe you.

For all it knows I'm
world without end, the Neptune
of upstate New York. (Just kidding.)
I get carried away by my own
conceits, constantly carried away . . .

HIS NICHE

Evasion was his specialty,
the long pause, the white space
on the page. What he didn't say
was wonderful. He was moved by
emptiness and the way invisible things
like air and love try to fill it.

He thought words expanded too
if left to themselves. He could say
"bell" and listen for hours.
He could say "cloud" and it would take
days to pass over his head.
And "moon." There were always
moons in his poems, blue-edged as whey,
melting into the night sky.

He loved the dark, fell asleep
dreaming he'd never wake up.
"Leaving," he loved its dying fall.
And "fading" and "fainting away."
He sought the shore for its blank
horizon. Life became, like the surf,
a petty din in his ears.

In the end they reduced his body
to pure white ash and praised him
as poet of absence, master of all
the vast, untented realm of possibility.

FARM KITTENS

My grandmother used to drown them in sacks.
They were stepped on, eaten by hogs,
discovered floating in rain barrels
or clogging drains. Or, ripe with scabs,
they simply died in secret places
under the porch, in the fields or barn.

Scrawny half-grown ones jostled each other
for a taste of whey and fought for scraps.
No hand gentled them. They used to hide
in the chicken coop, among the feed bags.
If I sat there long enough, sometimes
they crept out, cagey, in tantalizing

halos of fur. Their eyes bulged
like marbles. I wondered if they were blind.
Being a town child, I named them—
Snowball, Fluffy, Butterscotch—wanted to
hold them, stroke them into their lives,
drag them on by the scruff of the neck.

SUNFLOWERS

Painting the flowers is just
an excuse to keep on seeing them
as they open, curl, unwind
in their furtive
escape from summer's grid.

Your eyes are awash with changes
of green and gold.
Light drifts away;
there is always something
more to be felt and wished for.

You think about all you have learned
from their pebbly hearts,
going over the past with a soft brush—
blossom, leaf, stem—
till petals fall and the unmanageable
vision stays your hand.

for Fran Gillespie

THE SCHOLAR'S STONE GARDEN

From the moon pavilion, as from the prow
of a pleasure boat,
I view my garden of stones—still sea
on which I float through time.

When I see how slowly they grow, I am comforted.

Brush strokes on paper.
Stones scattered on sand.

I would be buried clutching a stone,
ticket of passage to that world,
proof of residence in this.

My parents were stones.

My wife is a stone of
ugly, intricate basalt.
Her hard breasts are teaching me
what I must know.

Our children are small, smooth stones
she found in the river.

I rake them. I water them,
stroke their sides, smooth as mushrooms,
dream of eating them one by one, till my belly
hangs down, pregnant with necessity.

My scrolls pile up like stones.

Who can say a stone has come to naught?
That it will not flower
after centuries of silence?

MAKE-UP

In the next room
my daughters are plotting
their escape
under cover of

"Tokyo Rose" and
"Iced Champagne."
Their lips are sticky
as lollipops.

When their new friend,
Maybelline,
waves a tiny wand,
they will be gone.

But I will leave first
by the back door,
wearing "Youth,"
my own disguise.

SAVING SIBERIA

Remember that morning you woke
to the whistle hooting, *No School, No School*?
Through frosty openings you saw
overnight you had landed in a glacial neighborhood.
No birds broke the dazzle.
Polar bears browsed in the shrubbery.

Oh, it was you, booted and scarved, stepped out
on the world's white throat to plant the flag;
you, who gathered the snow together till it rose
in a shining, slippery dome; you, alone
who hollowed it out like a pup,
for you knew at last what you were up to.

Meanwhile your mother discovered a driveway.
Plows laid out streets and sidewalks.
Snow slipped from branches with sickly plops
and little boys threw it at each other.
There is no stopping the rise of civilization.
But under the dome, nothing changed or gave way.
You feasted on ice, waiting for caribou.

for Nell

THE WATER-GARDEN, GIVERNY

(As if in the voice of Alice Hoschedé,
Claude Monet's second wife. His first wife,
Camille Doncieux, died at the age of 31.)

Claude, the lilies
are spreading their skirts
for bees and dragonflies. They remind me
of all our girls—Suzanne,
Blanche, Marthe, Camille—yes, even Camille
seems like one of them. She alone
has not grown stout and grey
but flits, mothlike,
over the garden in pale,
impeccable gowns,
her eyes averted or coyly masked
by violet silk, green leaves.

You said (I never forgot it) each leaf
was as important as each face.
I disagreed but understood;
she never did,
drifting relentlessly
over the poppies while you watched
her eyes grow murky like the pond
and added more viridian to your palette.

It has taken almost a lifetime but now,
at last, we have gone away—
she, I, even your Jean
(oh yes, I know you grieved).
There is no one left to keep you
from knowing that always
you loved light best, wooing it constantly
as it flared
across Argenteuil, Trouville,
the landscapes of our hats and parasols.

Today the odor of death
hangs over the lilies.
Perhaps even they would rather be loved
for themselves—not for their pallor,
tinged with chrome yellow, vermilion—
not for their small-gloved
fingers reaching
out with rare, diaphanous sighs.

VANISHING POINT

Right before you disappear
you find yourself in a Japanese
garden, all that's left
of the world, the one
you thought was here to stay.

And nothing remains of time
but a bamboo pole, filling with water
and tapping on stone. Those green
spires on the banks of the stream
that flows into the ground and seeps away
are little monuments to blue
that turned into kimonos and silk scarves.

There is one flute and a
tinny gong, a tiny priest to lead you
through horned gates.
In the teahouse a woman
warms her hands on a cup,
and for the time being the moon
is still a bridge.

SPRING FIRE

For two years we have avoided this log—
knotted, unsplittable, its origin unknown.
Gradually it has sunk to the bottom of the pile,
indeed, becomes the pile, to which we turn,
for the last time, this dank spring morning
after a night of rain. If it burns—when it burns,
it will heat the room for hours.

We prepare for it carefully, build up coals,
a small, hot fire, before we lay it on.
Old log, we salute you.
Outside it is green, green May and the
wren, the wren, the wren wrings her heart out.
Here it is winter still. I huddle by the hearth.

When the song begins I think first of birds—
the high, terse whistle of a chickadee, prolonged
beyond all natural endurance; a distant siren,
skidding towards disaster; a mosquito prematurely
sprung from the puddle underneath the swings.

I listen as the song winds on, high, sinuous
and sweet. It is the old log singing.
There is something green in its heartwood yet.
I hang on to that thread, that wheezy threnody.
I will learn its alphabet, translate
the jingling of acorns or pine cone bells,
the crack that tears trunk from stump. Together
we will write log-songs for rasps and musical saws.
But abruptly it stops as the log catches fire.

Now let the leaves take over, fretting like tambourines,
let flowers open with soft, lush sighs;
the sounds of summer will bury your warped whistle,
old asthmatic stick. When the sun returns
I will go out and sweep the patio clear
of splinters and bark. But now I lean forward
and warm my hands by your wild, burning side.

II THE SMOKE OF THE VILLAGES

LATE REPORT FROM MISS HARRIET ROBINSON'S THIRD GRADE

1. Waynesboro, Pennsylvania, 1948

This is the year we start fractions, learn
to cut a pie in any number of pieces,
but Gloria Creager and I can't figure out
how to divide the new boy in class.
At recess in bad weather we stay inside
and "Skip to My Lou" around the desks.
She and I fight to dance with Bobby Kribbs.
Sometimes she wins, sometimes I do.
She looks like Shirley Temple but I'm clever.
Whenever Miss Robinson has to leave the room,
I'm elected teacher.

                                        In our class picture
Miss Robinson, head cocked like a turkey hen,
keeps an eye on us. Gloria looks at Bobby,
who stares beyond the borders of the print,
his crew cut pale and thick as a puppy's ruff.
Already he's learned to dodge and feint. (His father
coaches the football team to loss after loss.)
Perhaps he knows they'll soon be leaving town,
is dreaming his father's early death, the years
he'll play the game, trying to be his father.

And me? I grin, standing beside him, eyes
closed against the flash or maybe already
a poem flutters behind translucent lids.
Over our heads the alphabet unwinds,
tendrils and loops twining around each other
in a script we are just beginning to understand.
This is the year I start to hate Gloria
forever, the year I refuse to wear leggings
anymore. A cold wind strokes my thighs,
lifts my skirt and smooths it back down.

2. Lewisburg, Pennsylvania, 1981

I am abroad in the world, lose track of everyone,
arrive one day in a place that looks like home
to read aloud my poems, my life. Afterwards
someone says, "Were you in Miss Robinson's class?"
He doesn't wax his hair these days, but I know him.
I've always been sure I would. "Bobby Kribbs!
Are you still unattached?" He shakes his head,
amused, and then, in the brief space of only
thirty-three years, I see he never loved me,
but raised his eyes by accident from the spelling book,
whirled past windows, chalk boards, closets, dutifully
clutching my sweaty hand.
                                        How loud I sang
so he would hear my voice above the rest.
"This time," Miss Smith, the music teacher, said,
"I want Jane Hess and Barbara West *not*
to sing." Was Freckle West a rival too?
Their names come back: Ronnie Zimmerman, who left
a candy bar on my desk each day (I ate it
too) till his mother got her grocery bill
at the end of the month; Truella Werking, who lost
a nickel and got us all kept in because
she said we'd stolen it; Alice and Phyllis Rowe,
whom I dismissed as liars because they claimed
they were twins (one was a midget, for heaven's sake).

For the first time I think of Harriet Robinson
as a woman about my age. I think of Bobby
walking home after the reading. It's late.
His daughter's room is dark, but a small light
glows by his wife's bed. She has fallen asleep.
Still, she needs to get under the covers. He rubs
her shoulder and whispers, "Gloria, guess what!"

UKIYO-E (Pictures of the Floating World)

Three laborers sat by the water,
listening to the water scour grey rocks,
watching a sickle moon mow green cliffs,
talking of mighty warriors.

Three warriors sat by the water,
listening to the water invade grey rocks,
watching a sickle moon pierce green cliffs,
talking of fabulous princes.

Three princes sat by the water,
listening to the water command grey rocks,
watching a sickle moon crown green cliffs,
talking of celebrated poets.

Three poets sat by the water,
listening to the water address grey rocks,
watching a sickle moon sketch green cliffs,
talking of august philosophers.

Three philosophers sat by the water,
listening to the water explain grey rocks,
watching a sickle moon probe green cliffs,
talking of common laborers.

Three by the water. Rocks, moon, cliffs.
So Katsushika Hokusai depicted them,
near Edo, under the Tokugawan rule,
during a peace that lasted 250 years.

MORNING AND WE ARE HOUSEHOLDERS

We begin at sundown, Yakup and I and the others,
carrying cinderblocks from Otto's place
where we have been hiding them for weeks,
waiting for a moonless night
when Baykal, the drunken one, is on patrol.

We pace the lot.
Some say it belongs to Saltik, the grape seller.
If so, it will serve him right
for weighing his thumb with the fruit.
We pace the lot, or rather, Yakup does,
as if he were once again preparing the ground for seed.
How much can we take in a night?
Will we have room for a beast in cold weather?
Quickly the men begin laying the first row.
The women mix mortar and show me how
to slap it in place. They say
they have helped others before us.

In the country we lived in a mud hut
my grandfather built himself.
It was a proper dwelling, with thick walls
of brick baked in the sun for many days.
While I was still too young for baggy pants
we had a tree, though the goats had eaten its bark
beyond a man's height, and a well
that gave sweet water.
My mother had two gold teeth
which she sold for my dowry.
It is better now for her to be dead
but we must go on, Yakup and I.

As we lay the last roof tiles, the sun comes up,
glinting off the guns that always point
this way from the opposite hill
on which another town rises,
its houses, like those around us, stuccoed
in shades of pink, blue, green, and gold.

Both here and there women are waking early.
Soon the lanes will be full of chickens and geese
and schoolchildren in smocks with white collars.
In the teahouses men will gather
to smoke, play dominoes. Tomorrow I
will gossip beside the stream.
I will wrap my head in a gay scarf
and plaster our walls with some bright color too—
a wildflower in the mountain pass.

AFTER MANET

After Manet came Monet.
("This is a joke!" raged Edouard,
when they complimented him on "his" seascapes
at the Academy.) And after Monet
stubbornly sacrificed everything for light,
came Sisley, Renoir, Degas, Morisot; came
Cézanne and wild Van Gogh, the engines, the lilies.

After Manet even you and I
could give up masquerades. We appeared
in ordinary dress with sleeves rolled up or
took off our clothes and bathed
in speckled shade, eyes focused
on the indistinguishable future and past.
We learned, after Manet, to analyze
the scarlet traces in the bullring's dust.

And after that
the line that separated us from each other
and from the rest of the world
became blurred / was recognized
as fiction after all. And ordinary sadness,
in delicate shades of peach or plum,
descended upon our very real lives.

TWIGS

Let's go out
and gather some.
When we put them in water they bloom.
When we light them
they fill the room
with resinous laughter.

Here is what happened when twigs were young.
A rabbit ate them. Deer ate them.
A dog pissed and they shriveled.
But some escaped and vowed
to rebuild.

Twigs have their secrets,
a script we can't unravel,
songs so quiet only the buds
hear and sway.

These are the uses of twigs:
to make a nest, to tease a pig,
to brush your teeth (if you chew the tips),
to toss in a brook, to brew for tea,
to build little ladders
other twigs can climb.

Trunks are led upward by twigs,
the forerunners, they who
reach out, who are unafraid of heights.

Most of the sky has been claimed by them.
Only a few uncharted spots
remain over sand, water, asphalt.

Every spring the twigs want leaves,
but then they tire of them.

In the wind an old oak
shakes its twigs
like a stag at mating time.

MAGIC

Somewhere a ship is tilling the sea.
And somewhere in the shape of a ship
four girls sit, scarcely breathing,
lest the wind rise, scarcely moving,
lest the ship pitch and toss.
One dreams of the side of the ship
where the sun comes up, another
of the side where it descends.
One feels the spume sting her face,
another lingers over the wake.

They must not eat rice in coconut milk
or the ship will stick in the water.
They must not, for a moment, think
of their lovers, or the ship will be
lured onto rocks. They neither speak
nor sing. At all times one is awake,
her hands clasped over her breasts
to steady the mariner's grasp.

Even after the ship arrives,
with its cargo of copra and cinnabar,
at some luminous haven, the girls
must not eat fish with sharp bones,
lest the return be delayed. They must
carry themselves through the village streets
as if their bones were coral or jade.
As if their hands were flowers
opening, closing at the bottom of the sea.

THE UNDOING

"In the island of Saghalien, when a woman is in labour,
her husband undoes everything that can be undone."
—Frazer, *The Golden Bough*

Husband, spit out thy bread,
untie thy shoes.
Draw bungs from casks,
raise windows, unlock doors.
Unlatch the barnyard gate,
let cows drift into the orchard
to gorge on green apples.
Loose Dobbin's bridle,
scatter the geese like summer snow.

Have you opened all drawers
and cupboards? Unstopped drains?
Have you freed the dog?
Is the boat sailing itself away
from the mooring slip?
Has the bird fled its cage?
The roast escaped from the oven?

Take the axe from its stump.
Take pins from the sheets
on the line. Let them fly
over the fence or into the trees,
let them hover like angels. Oh,
husband, there is a time
for the tying of knots and a
time for breaking them.

See, I have undone my apron strings,
unbraided my hair,
unbuttoned my gown. Now,
now, I am learning
how everything yearns to be free,
must be so.

TANTE FRÄNI'S HANDKERCHIEF

Here is Tante Fräni's handkerchief.
Her fingers do this, and this,
folding and tugging and knotting until,
from a fist of linen, *voilà*!
a little white mouse with lace whiskers
quivers in her palm.
His magnificent tail droops over her wrist.
His pointy ears tilt this way and that
for the sound of laughter—that's what he likes.
He's a natural clown, but nervous.
His body is stuffed with giggles.

"We are going to do a trick for the children,"
says Tante. He makes a false start.
"No, no," she scolds. "Not till I say so.
You must relax, calm down."
She strokes his tail and whispers in his ear.
He whispers back but she shakes her head.
"Not today," she says sternly.
He whispers again. She nods.
"Perhaps, if you do it right."

He gathers himself together, almost stops quivering.
Tante Fräni says, "Not yet . . . not yet . . . now!"
And the marvelous white handkerchief leaps
high over the children's hands and heads.
As a reward it will be permitted
to hide in Tante Fräni's drawer
beside the lavender sachet.
And tomorrow, for love of her,
it will become a cradle or a rose.

ICE AGE

In the days before home freezers
my parents rented a locker
at the Waynesboro Ice
and Cold Storage Company.
I often went there in the evening
with my father to get a chunk of something—
petrified rib roast, sliced peaches in amber.
I thought of getting locked up by mistake
behind the padded door in a perpetual glare,
while my flesh grew marbled
and my toes fell off. A few nights later
someone (my father, perhaps, coming back
for sausage or hamburger)
would find me, a frosted woolly cake.
But he would press his lips to mine
and take me into his arms—and every time,
we stepped back into the jungle, yes,
in Pennsylvania, in mid-winter.

YOUR NAME IN GREEK

Your name in Greek reminds me
of goat bells,
calling me to the hills.

Your French name has a shifty
sound, like half-full baggage cars.

In Swedish it suggests
pickled onions, salt fish on toast.
In Spanish it smothers me.

In Hebrew it sounds like "peace."
It's on everyone's lips.
I'm jealous.

I'm afraid of your Russian name.
Your Arabic one gives me the jitters.

In Hungarian it's a cough
caught in the throat.

And if it exists elsewhere,
in China, Andromeda,
someday I too will arrive.

THE CITY OF CARDS

There is no weather here,
only the silent drift of day and night.
We never touch and
speak only in whispers, hand over mouth,
to shield the delicate walls from collapse.
Even the Japanese, with their mats
and rice paper screens,
never went this far—to live so
fragilely, with such restraint.
And yet, works of great beauty
(temples, monuments, cloisters,
the Palace of Hearts itself)
have been known to vanish overnight.
Daily the maze must be rebuilt.
You could never escape that way.

KILLING HARVEST

We moved as an army,
swinging our scythes like noisemakers.
Ripe heads burst under our boots.
Our bodies grew red from exertion.
As we closed in from all sides
the standing crop dwindled
until it occupied little more
than the space of a man.
The last swath fell to me.

I swung without thinking and felt,
or thought I felt,
the stalks resist my blade.
The others laughed, "Ha, ha!
Time for the old man to die."
Afterwards we bathed in the river,
rinsing away the heat and dust.
But a strange odor still clung to me.

And during the days of rejoicing
only I was silent,
who could have told them
there was no old man. He was young,
with eyes like those blue flowers
that spring up quickly after the rain.

THE BUTTER ROAD

It is everything that occurs to you—
treacherous, tantalizing—
that shimmer in the sun
is no mirage but the pure
stuff, waiting for pancakes.

I wouldn't lie to you,
not about Pennsylvania.
Neither would my father,
who says he turns thirteen again
every time he walks along
the Butter Road, whistling.

His mother still needs a
little something from the store,
though she's been dead now
almost twenty years.
She doesn't lie either.

That's how it is with us
country folk. Have I ever
told you about the rivers of cider,
the abattoirs of cake?

SPECIAL FRIENDS

The first day of school Miss Blessing
called a big, mean-looking kid
to the front of the room and put her
arm around him. "Class," she said,
"I'd like you to meet my special friend,
Donny Rowe. He's come back to spend
another year in first grade with me."
Donny squirmed and tried to pick his nose.
Already his hair was mussed.
He was growing out of his overalls.

Even now when I think of villains, Donny
comes to mind. He teased girls.
He talked back. He never knew the answer
to anything. It wasn't long before
he got his first beating and came back
grinning from the dark hall of coats
and boots. (Donny never wore boots,
and coats only when it suited him.)

Miss Blessing was always breaking rulers,
she hit him that hard, or so I was told
by my special friend, a small red-headed girl,
who swore up and down her name was
Nancy *Fire-Pumpkin* Bain.

THE EVERGLADES

What the sea gives with one hand,
with the other it takes back,
like you and me,
building reefs and tearing them down.
I see us in the mangroves too, swallowing tears,
learning to live on salt water.

Herons preen on brittle legs, ignoring
hunters, fishermen, us.
Anhingas hang up their wings to dry
on islands rising from oceans of grass.
A small raccoon nibbles wild plums by the road.

From the shore, with its shell gatherers,
its maze of pelicans shifting in the sky,
we move out to deep water,
away from bleached sand, rock
hammered to dust.

What we thought would be pure fun
is rather like watching the duck
swim over the alligator.
I get sick in the glass-bottomed boat
while you are happily counting barracuda.
But you don't like it either when the rudder breaks.

Still, jellyfish rise like soap bubbles;
clownfish clown. You put your arm around me
and we are rescued at last
by a circus of small craft.

You may question the words "rescued" and
"happily," tell me how supple
a bird's legs really are,
which is to say, "my Florida," "your Florida"—
congruent realms that sometimes touch.

MODEL VICTORY

A battleship has run
aground on the patio, after a
frightful voyage
through the chrysanthemums.
For months it foundered
in the sandbox, was beached
on sticks and stones,
then sucked up at last
in a vortex of flying leaves.

Now if it can just make it
through the door and rise, somehow,
to the playroom, with what joy
the patchwork hippopotami, the Bavarian
bears, the dolls and mice, the
miniature veterans
will greet it,
home from the south,
from the monstrous model wars.

for Ben

AUGUST PHILOSOPHERS

"Be generous," says the loosestrife,
flinging its coarse silks over the grass.

"Move on," says the stream
through a mouthful of silt.

Across the road a little music school
opens its doors and windows to summer.

And seven children with shiny flutes
play *do,* then *re,* then *mi.*

PEACETIME

The year I started school
my grandfather died and I
got my tonsils out and my
cat moved in next door
with some people named Schultz.
We bought a new black car
and stopped calling our
yard a "victory garden."
And everyone who was coming
home from the war came home
and my mother's belly rose
like raw dough.

Suddenly, in her eighth
month her mouth went
crooked. They rushed her
to the hospital and
Mary came to keep house for us.
"I'll have to do it my way,"
she said and fussed
with her little moustache.
She was ageless and dark,
with braided hair, maybe part Indian.
Dad and I still talk
about the boiled dandelion
greens we pushed around our plates,
trying to get used to her "ways"
in the kitchen. She slept
with me and had her own way
of going to bed too, crept
around in the dark and wore
her nightgown over long-legged,
fuzzy underwear. She snored
and said I ground my teeth
in my sleep—
a sure sign of worms.

Once she took me to her farm
to see the rabbits. They were warm
and made soft squeaky

sounds and nibbled leaves
from my hand, forcing
their noses through the mesh.
She raised them for food.
I wanted one. (I missed the cat.)
Maybe that was why, when Dad
came home early one day
and said, "Janie,
guess what. Mommy had
twin boys this morning!"
I jumped around braying,
"One for you and one for me!"

That was peacetime
and the end of it.
Just the two of us, jumping
up and down.

for Kate

REFUGEES

They say they like it here, in New Jersey.
There is something to think about, something to do
with your hands.
The seasons excite them.
They love feeling restless again
after millenniums of beatitude.

As I look out the window I see them
clipping the hedge and mowing the grass.
They move more quickly these days, with an almost
harried gait.
Their wings are no longer white, but dove
grey or soft, dusty brown.

THAT RECENT INVENTION, THE WHEEL

Grandma didn't invent the wheel.
Walnut Street was too steep.
She may have invented God.
For sure, she invented marriage to my grandfather,
who invented hardware stores and
everything that's in them—all the
screws and nails, cup hooks, tools, wallpaper,
giant spools of wire and twine.
He may have thought, once or twice, if only
one were to turn those spools sideways,
how far they would go, but at that point,
a customer always turned up.

My mother, bless her heart, invented wash day
and spring cleaning and Sunday dinner and
good manners and the proverb:
"Hoe your own row." My father
invented the moon, which he promised her
on those crisp fall evenings when
they were inventing love.

My husband invented the cello and dessert.
Our daughter came up with infancy, the triangle,
and household pets. It was up to me,
midlife, to invent the wheel.
I was not, as some have suggested, trying to
transport a flatbed on rolling logs,
or construct the pyramids. It was just
an idea I got from watching children
tumble down a grassy slope, and then there was
the way beads rolled off
when my necklace broke. After that came roads
and places to go. You know the rest.

This morning over breakfast
our sons, who invented the bicycle,
faced each other with such hatred in their eyes,
it is only a matter of time
until they think of murder
and flight.

THE PLEASURE OF THIS DANCE

1. In the Pergola

In the pergola a woman is dancing.
Her bare feet slap the bricks.

She has laid her robe aside
and dances in halter and slip.

Her gauze slip flares as she raises
first one leg and then the other.

Her arms meet overhead
like the handle of a basket.

She turns left towards the orchard
and right towards the forsythia,

drifting away from the house,
away from the picket fence.

Her hair uncoils, snakes down her back,
casting a twisted shadow on the floor.

As she sways in green pergola light
her eyes close, or so it seems,

and rain begins on the roof of leaves,
buds tremble like plucked strings.

2. The Invitation

Her white head ducks under his arm.
He smiles sweetly, counting to himself
like a man laying bricks. "Why have we never done
this before?" they ask, breaking into
The Cross-over, The Invitation.

Mostly they dance in the kitchen,
over linoleum tulips, past the oven, the sheer
sides of the refrigerator. Or waltz,

half-humming, into the living room
with its carpet of roses, or perhaps

Evening has come, and they sway upstairs
among the monumental bureaus and beds,
where the memory of children, heavy-headed, persists.
"Mother, Father!" we cry over the dark music
pouring from curtains, treetops, mottled sky.

3. Danse Macabre

I used to stomp
caterpillars, loved
the smack
of small bubbles
bursting under my
sandals and the splashed
pus and bile.

I fed the cat
butterflies
and I kept lightning
bugs in jars
till their green
fire went out.

I stomped ants too, and
slugs—patter, squish!
patter, squish! Till the
sidewalk was slippery
and dangerous.

4. *Mai Ogi (An Eighteenth-Century Fan)*

From the box of fans she selects one,
not *akome ogi,* the one her mother
takes to Court to hide her teeth,
not *gun sen,* grandfather's ancient battle fan,
with its blades of wrought iron, not
riki ogi, auntie's fan for passing
little tea cakes in the ceremony,
but *mai ogi,* the dancing fan,
because she is young and feels like dancing.

Slowly she opens the gilded sky,
causing the moon to rise and grow full
over grass fine as her hair.
A few pink blossoms appear.
All is landscape, anticipation. Then,
from behind the last ivory blade,
a small bird pops out, bearing her name.
She is the daughter of Sakai Hoitsu,
painter of fans for the emperor himself.
But he has made this one for her.
She raises it above her head and turns,
creating her own gay breeze.

5. *Pas de Deux*

First the mouse dances.
Then they dance together.
Then the cat dances alone.

6. I Have Beheld Such Splendors

Ababa, Bird Woman, does not dance
in Central Park on summer afternoons,
eyes closed, among the pigeons,
in her garments flimsy as down, to whatever
the radio plays—jazz, rock, the news.

She does not nod her head, bound
with a dung-colored scarf,
on her long old neck to the girl on skates,
the man with whippets, the man with a cigar.

Of these things she has been accused,
but no—

She heaves herself through air,
by means of her skinny brown arms,
like a swimmer, surfacing above the pines,
above the brick and stone, in a place
where cranes move to the slow tune of silence.

She bows to her partner, the tall, mottled one.
They drift towards each other, tendons
braced, breasts and thighs straining for grace
in the ancient, sacred display.

Ababa, Bird Woman, does not sleep
in doorways, nested in rags. She does not eat
what she finds in refuse heaps,
in alleyways, crumbs from the street.
I tell you, she returns to the sun
and puts on her kimono of fire.

THE JUNIPER PRIZE

This volume is the eighth recipient
of the Juniper Prize,
presented annually by the
University of Massachusetts Press
for a volume of original poetry.
The prize is named in honor of Robert Francis,
who has lived for many years at
Fort Juniper, Amherst, Massachusetts.